Alicia J Evans

How I Got Over
My Journey on Overcoming Loss

Alicia J Evans

Alicia J Evans

WIND BENEATH MY WINGS
PUBLISHING

Copyright © 2023 Alicia J Evans

All rights reserved.

ISBN: 979-8-9852349-3-0
Online versions of the Bible-KJV, GN, NIL

Alicia J Evans

DEDICATION

I dedicate this book to my parents, Leroy & Jural Evans, my grandmother Minnie Pollard, my Aunt Rolene Flournoy, my Aunt Edith & Uncle Issac Blake. To my siblings, Anthony, Doreather, and Mattie, may you each continue to be the wind beneath my wings.

Alicia J Evans

ACKNOWLEDGMENTS

I would like to acknowledge God because without him in my life I truly do not know where I would be.

The wonderful members of Sugar & Spice Book Club Thank You all.

Robin Devonish your writing workshop guided me on this writing project many years ago.

Yvonne Kong-Eusebe, once again sis you are the big sister that is always on point.

And, to my family and friends whose life and death gave me the strength to share my journey. I pray to see your faces again.

Last but never least, Nathaniel, Thank you for always believing in me and pushing me to put my thoughts down on paper.

Alicia J Evans

This book was in my heart to write after the loss of my mother in 2008. Jural Evans, was my mother, my friend, and my road dog. She was more women than I could ever dream to be. Not until I was a grown woman myself did I realize and understand how much of a remarkable mother and woman she was. My mother lived her life on her own terms with no regrets.

My mother's brief fight with breast cancer and then inevitable death left me with a feeling of loss and helplessness. Well to be honest, it was a strong feeling of loss. At, the time I also had an overwhelming feeling and desire to give up.

If I am being transparent my struggle with loss and attempting to get over it, did not begin with my mother's passing but actually with my fathers.

In 1995 I lost my father, Leroy Evans Sr. He loved his children. He instilled in me the importance of family and commitment to family. My father's determination in giving his children something to hold on to, like traditions and being proud of your heritage are true lifetime nuggets.

My father died from cancer as well. His fight was short and untimely. His passing less than two months after his diagnosis left me hurt, confused and distraught.

Then a mere three years later in 1998 my oldest sister passed away. My sister Doreather [Reecie] was the gem of big sisters. She was the epitome of a true sister friend. She knew me better than I knew myself. She was always willing to offer encouragement when needed. She also knew how to step back and allow you to make your mistakes and would be there to catch you when you fall.

"Reecie" as she was affectionately known, was diagnosed with scleroderma at an early age. She passed away when she was in her thirties from lung cancer. Which is one of the side effects of this disease.

I was determined to be there for her in her time of need. I knew that I could not let her down. Burying my oldest sister while I was still grieving the loss of my father was too much for me to handle.

But guess what? Each day I wake up and realize I am still here.

I just have to wonder *How I Got Over*.

My decision to write *How I Got Over* was not a selfish one. I am hoping that by sharing what has helped me, I can in turn help others. What we need to remember each day is that He did not bring us this far to leave us.

So please read and be strengthened as I am each time I read through these pages.

How I Got Over

When you are stuck in a situation and you finally have a breakthrough, a feeling of joy engulfs you.

I love the comparison of getting over as a breakthrough. A parting of dark clouds and moving into the beautiful sunlight.

When you are in the midst of the darkness of losing a loved one, you may not believe you will get over this sadness.

One of the things I have come to realize is that God gives you what you need in your time of need.

He has given us a tool that we can use anytime we become a little doubtful.

I was brought up in a Baptist church. I attended

bible study on Friday evenings and Sunday school on Sunday mornings. During those times I was taught many lessons of the bible. Throughout those classes I was taught how to pray and prayer changes things.
So, when life gets hard we must lean on our first line of defense.

The Lord's Prayer

Our Father which art in heaven, hallowed be thy name.
Thy kingdom come, Thy will be done on earth as it is in heaven.
Give us this day our daily bread and forgive us our debts as we forgive our debtors.
And lead us not into temptation, but deliver us from evil: For thine is the kingdom, and the power, and the glory, for ever
Amen
Matthew 6: 9-13-KJV

Never Alone

When I was faced with some of life's struggles, like burying both parents and older siblings, I forgot all that I was taught. Well not so much that I forgot but I felt God had turned his back on me.

I knew in my heart and soul all the bible verses told me He will not leave me nor forsake me.

I know he is a mother to the motherless and a father to the fatherless. The hardest thing was to wrap my mind over all I knew to be true and to what was happening in my life.

There were days when I could not pray because I felt like my prayers were going unanswered.

In the days I felt alone and betrayed, I was resistant to the gospel truth that God was working in my life, even then.

In our darkest hour God promises to never leave us. He promised to send his comforter the Holy Ghost. I am also sure that he places family and friends in our life to help strengthen us and to hold us up when we feel we may fall.

When we feel like God has forgotten and forsaken us, rest assure it is at these times he is working his hardest on our behalf. There is a saying you have friends in your life for a season and a reason. Mourning is one of the seasons we may go through in life. You may go through this season numerous times throughout your lifetime. And it is at these times you can understand the meaning of his words "I promise to leave you never alone."

On the day that my father died, God used my young nephew to remind me that he was there in the midst of it all.

My father passed away in the house. The funeral home directors came to collect the body from the house. They allowed everyone to say their goodbyes. I was the last one, I guess because I was the only one that had not accepted my father's illness. As I was sitting by his body I remembered crying out "why did you leave me." I was crying saying, "I have no one and I would be all alone and who would take care of me now." In my despair I felt arms around me holding me and comforting me. It was my nephew who was fifteen at the time. With his arms around me I recall hearing him say, "I am here Aunt Leisha, I will always take care of you."

*"So with you: Now is your time of grief,
but I will see you again and you will
rejoice, and no one will take
away your joy"*
John 16:22 KJV

*"Fear, thou not for I am with thee,
be not dismayed; for I am thy God;
I will strengthen thee; yeah I will
help thee
yeah I will uphold thee with the right
hand of my righteousness"*
Isaiah 41:10 KJV

*"And I will pray the Father, and he shall
Give you another Comforter,
That he may abide with you forever"*
John 14:16 KJV

*"I will not leave you comfortless:
I will come to you"*
John 14:18 KJV

What I am thankful and forever grateful for is My God knew what I needed. He was not angry when I turned a deaf ear to him. My deaf ear came in the form of not going to church on Sunday mornings or refusing the communion cup on the First Sunday of the month.

He was the ever-loving father that always had my best interest at heart. I did like I am sure many of you have done, when faced with the death of loved ones we turn away from God. Turning away from God does not mean that you or I are nonbelievers. What it means is that we have a right to ask God "has he forsaken us? " And with that in mind we know that he has placed family and friends in our lives to help us deal with life struggles.

Never Alone

At the times when I felt my lowest
My very weakest
Never Alone
In the quiet midnight hours
Never Alone
Not the one day I sat by your bedside
Never Alone
Not even the night I signed the papers to have
the tubes removed
Never Alone
Even when I looked in your eyes and whispered
in your ear "Thank You"
as you took your last breath
Never Alone
Through the pain
Through the tears

How I Got Over

Never Alone
Heart aches, and heart breaks
Never Alone
When you feel the wind against your face
When you hear a whisper in your ear
I am there
That warm feeling that engulfs you, that chill that makes you shudder
I am there
He promises to never leave you or forsake you
Take his hand and he will carry you through
-Alicia J Evans

When my sister passed away I remember thinking, okay, I did good this time. I had accepted her illness. Did my sisterly duties by going to the hospital every day. I was sure that God was going to answer all my prayers and make her well. What I knew for certain was that my big sister was not going to die. Not now.

See, she was the one that held it together for everyone else. She was the one that you would go to for all your problems. She was the secret keeper. And she would not once be judgmental. What she did do was want you to be the best that you could be. As I think back to the type of sister she was. I am reminded of a time she had me sign a contract that I would finish school. I was not going to class and thinking that I did not have to go to school. She knew that education was very important to helping me become the women I was meant to be. So, she did what only my big sister would do. I believe, in her mind she knew if she got my signature on a piece of paper it would be binding, and she could hold me to that promise of completing my education.

How ironic, I would be the one to have to sign the paper to remove the breathing tube which was keeping her alive. It felt like my signature on that form was a binding contract between my sister and me. My sister, who enjoyed life and all that it had to offer, could not speak for herself so I had to represent her. I was convinced Reecie would not want to live while a machine was breathing for her.

It is with that same binding contract in my mind that inspired me years later to finally complete my education.

Even with this understanding I still found myself asking the questions again.

Why would you put this on me?

Why have you forsaken me?

Why did you leave me here to deal with this all alone?

Not even her favorite scripture helped me at this time. Hebrews 11:1,

Now, faith is the substance of things hoped for, the evidence of things not seen.

But what did help me was the gospel song my sister sung at our father's funeral.

Order my steps in Your word dear Lord,
lead me, guide me every day,
send Your anointing, Father I pray;
order my steps in Your word,
please, order my steps in Your word.
Humbly, I ask Thee to teach me Your will,
while You are working, help me be still,
Satan is busy, but my God is real;
order my steps in Your word,

please, order my steps in Your word.
Author Unknown

    I would picture her singing that song and it was then I realized my steps were being ordered.

    So once again I am thinking *How I Got Over*. It is not by my own design, through it all I am still here. Everyone goes through various stages of grieving, but we are all left with the burning question;

    Why my loved one?

    Before you get over one thing, then bam, you are hit with another devastating blow. I remember thinking, how much can one person bear?

He Knows How Much You Can Bear

Heartbreak, loneliness,
Sickness, death
He knows how much you can bear.
Confusion, disappointments
When your load seems heavy and the burdens
too much to bear
When you feel like giving up and nothing seems
to be going your way
Stay steadfast, unmovable, do not waiver.
Call on the one who promised to carry you
through.
He would not give you more than you can
handle.
He knows how much you can bear.
      -Alicia J Evans

Alicia J Evans

He Will Never Give You More Than You Can Bear

    I believe God will never give you more than you can bear. He knows you. He made you. He has numbered each hair on your head. He has placed things in your life that you can get strength from.
    You have the tools to make it. The bible teaches us that if we follow his word and teachings we will be all right. Just when you think you cannot go on or come to the end of your rope. When you

are in such despair that you are screaming enough is enough. It is now that your faith kicks in and keeps you going.

At times when I was at my weakest I am reminded of the story of Job. Job had lost it all and his body was struck with sickness. All of his family and friends begged him to curse his God. They tried to convince Job that what kind of God would take everything from him. That would make him suffer the way he was suffering. Through it all Job refused to curse God. Job knew how good God had been to him. Job knew that God giveth and God taketh.

God knew no matter what he allowed the devil to do in Job's life that his servant Job will not turn from him.

After losing my father, then three years later losing my oldest sister. And then just when I felt like I was dealing with those two life-changing deaths my mother passed away. I felt like I could not do every day mundane things like getting out of bed. The little things like bathing and eating had become too hard of a task for me to do on a daily basis.

And before I could heal my uncle, another sister and one of my brothers passed away. Surely I was living my Job story.

I felt like losing both parents, both sisters and a brother was way too much for even me. Me, who claims to be strong, me, who can handle it all, was definitely hitting a low point.

And it was then, I was reminded of the three

Hebrew boys in the fire, Daniel as he was faced with the lion, and David when he came up against Goliath.

So surely if I just looked up to the heavens and call on the name of Jesus for my strength I will come out on the other side.

Even though I have read and heard the 23rd Psalm many times, I had to go through some stuff to really understand what it means. It has become the scripture that I find myself repeating over and over on a daily basis. I now understand why it was my father's favorite scripture.

The Lord is my shepherd; I shall not want.
He maketh me to lie down in green pastures; he leadeth me beside still waters.
He restoreth my soul; he leadeth me in the paths of righteousness for his name sake
Yea, though I walk through the valley of the shadow of death,
I will fear no evil; for thou art with me; thy rod and thy staff they comfort me.
Thou preparest a table before me in the presence of mine enemies;

*thou anointest my head with oil; my cup
runneth over.
Surely, goodness and mercy shall follow me all
the days of my life; and I will
dwell in the house of the lord for ever
(Psalm 23) KJV*

What grieving has taught me, is you must hold on to what works. What worked for me was my faith. Even when I thought I had none. I am always reminded that God will not leave you nor forsake you. He keeps reminding us that he is and always will be there for us.

I am always reminded to pray in season, out of season. I was taught to pray with conviction.

As my former pastor the late Reverand Archie Witsell taught me way back in 1985, when my family was dealing with my Aunt Rolene's fight with cancer and ultimate death. Rev. Witsell would say, "pray until it feels like the ground under you is giving and you are sinking, and you have been knocked to your knees."

It is on your knees that you will find peace. On your knees you will feel God working over your life. On your knees you will find the strength to overcome that which you thought had you bound.

I love the feeling when you realize God is working to turn things around. Even in grief he is working for our good. In the mist of all the pain of losing a loved one God is working to bring you out of it stronger and better

Alicia J Evans

Stronger Than You Think

You can make it. In this moment, this thing that you are going through, right now you can make it. This pain is only a test. He has created you in his own image. You have what it takes to go through this stronger and better.

One day while we were talking, I asked my friend Yvonne, "why me, why am I the only one that can see my mother's body deteriorating?"

"Why do I have to be the one trying to hold everyone else up?"

And the reply I received was, "because your mother knew you would be the only one who could be strong enough to take care of it all and everyone."

That is like our heavenly father. He knows that you are stronger than the tears that will not stop falling.

He knows if we stay grounded, stay rooted, strong winds may blow, and bellows may roll, but he will keep us steady and upright. He will not let us fall.

He knows we may bend a little. We may even drop to our knees. But God knows your pain.

We are reminded that even on the cross his son Jesus whom he created had become a little shaken "if it is your will then let this cup pass from me."

God did not think Jesus was not strong, he allowed him to have that feeling. The burden he was carrying was maybe too much for even him to bear.

In that very moment Jesus realizing that his purpose in life was for this very moment. He accepted his life, bowed his head, and died.

When in your life you are faced with some of life's darkest hours, and you do not think you can make it another day. Remember God has a purpose for your life. It is not an option for us to give up. We have too much to live for. We have yet to live to our fullest potential.

You may not see the light at the end of the tunnel but believe me when I say, "if you keep pushing forward you will make it through to the light."

I am a living testimony that joy, sweet joy

comes in the morning. If you are anything like me, I know you are thinking you want joy now. You cannot wait until morning.

You are so much stronger than you give yourself credit for. You will make it through this storm. Hold on to his unchanging hand. Let the unconditional love of God engulf you and carry you through this storm.

*"But those who hope in the Lord will renew their strength
They will soar on wings like eagles; they will run*

*and not grow weary,
they will walk and not be faint."*
Isaiah 40:31 GNB

*"But he said to me "My grace is sufficient for you, for my power is made perfect in weakness". Therefore, I will boast all the more gladly about my weakness, so that Christ's power may rest on me.
That is way for Christ's sake, I delight in weakness, in insults, in hardships, in persecutions, in difficulties. For when I am weak, then I am strong."*
2 Corinthians 12: 9-10 GNB

In 2016 my sister Mattie (Bunnie) passed away. Once again it was quick and swift. And felt like it came out of nowhere.

I visited Bunnie in the hospital on Monday then on Tuesday my nephew called me to inform me his mother had told the doctors to stop all testing and she just wants to be made comfortable.

This news came as a shock to me because the night before she was still screaming and demanding they treat her.

In my despair I found a sense of peace in believing "Bunnie" had a talk with Jesus during the night and she was fine with what he showed her. I can only imagine as a believer my sister understood the gift in store for her with her dying, which is the gift of eternal life.

Understanding this has helped me when I have many sleepless nights missing my sister.

The peace I speak of does not come easy nor does it minimize the grieving process. What it does for me, and I hope for you, is it gives us something to look forward to. We can believe that this pain will not last long.

Grief is not reserved only for family members, it can also be detrimental when the loss applies to a friend. A few years ago, I lost a dear friend. Her death came as a shock. She was not sick, nor did she suffer from any underlining conditions. When you think of the saying, "here today and gone tomorrow" her passing was precisely that.

At the time I was fortunate enough to work with her brother and one morning when I arrived at work he informed me his sister was found unresponsive in her house. She was on the phone with another girlfriend when she stopped talking and responding to her friend. The friend became concerned and called 911. When they found her she had suffered a brain aneurysm. Enroute to the hospital she suffered multiple strokes.

I was at a loss for words as he was informing me of all the details. My heart was breaking, and I was trying to comprehend everything he was saying. My friend Tracey (not her real name) and I had not talked in a while because life had been getting in the way. The most recent phone call we shared ended it like always by promising to see each other soon.

After work I rushed to the hospital in Brooklyn. I needed to see her for myself. I was not allowing myself to believe this was happening to my friend. On the ride from the Bronx to Brooklyn I remember praying this is not true. This could not be true. Tracey is young, too young to be suffering this way.

Once I arrived at the hospital, I could not find

parking. I drove around for what seemed like an hour but all the while in communication with her brother who was keeping me updated on Tracey's condition. The last call from Tracey's brother was to tell me he did not want me to come into the hospital. He informed me her condition was not improving. Tracey's body was shutting down and she no longer looked like herself. Her brother said, "go home, I don't want you to see her like this, it is not good."

I recall thinking God knows me. He knows it would have destroyed me seeing Tracey in that condition. He was guiding me that night. Unable to find parking was his way of delaying my entrance into the hospital so I could receive the call from her brother.

The grief of losing my friend was different from losing a parent but the hurt was real. My heart was broken for all the laughs and conversations we will not get to have. The secrets that only friends share go untold.

Again, I had to lean on the source of my strength and what I encourage you to do when faced with a similar situation.

*"The Lord is near to the brokenhearted
and saves the crushed in spirit"*
Psalm 34:18 GNB

*"My flesh and my heart faileth: but God
Is the strength of my heart, and my
portion forever"*
Psalm 73:26 GNB

*"He heals the brokenhearted and
binds up their wounds"*
Psalm 147:3 GNB

I'm Still Here

I'm Still Here
Through the tears and the fears
I'm still here.
Through the broken heart, the hurt and pain
I'm still here.
Through the doubt
I'm still here.
Only through his grace and mercy
Stronger and Better
I'm still here.
-Alicia J Evans

Precious Memories

The late Reverand James Cleveland sung it best "Precious Memories oh how they linger. Forever invading my soul." When we find ourselves missing our loved ones memories of happier times help us to get over the rough days. Our memories are pictures or snapshots of our life. We use the snapshots to playback the life that we shared with our loved one.

Remembering a person's smile. The special way they laughed. The way only that person can do something. Memories in the early stages of losing a loved one can increase the feeling of loss. Making the loss that much more unbearable. Realization that they are no longer here to share in the process of creating memories but instead, has become a memory.

I remember after losing my father going to our church was very hard for me. I could not sit in the pew without recollecting seeing my father sitting on the pulpit. I could not keep myself from seeing him preaching a sermon. I would see him walking around the church, which he liked to do whenever he had on a new suit. He would always say "Sister so and so, said I sure looked good today" He would then ask, "Did you see me this morning?" My reply would be "Yes each of the three times you walked around" we would then both crack up laughing.

Remembering those moments and the many other times would send me into a state of depression. Not wanting to believe that my father was no longer here.

When others were celebrating the holidays and special occasions I would fall into a dark deep hole of loneliness. I would think there was no way to escape this unhappiness. And I would start wondering if I would ever enjoy the holidays or any special occasion again.

Then one day without me even noticing it happened. The memories did not cause pain. I was able to remember a time when; I was able to remember what they would say or do at certain times.

Those same memories that caused me pain were now giving me strength to go on. I would play back the pictures in my head. At one time I would cry, at simple thoughts of my loved ones, but now I can laugh at things that they did or said.

It is also at times like this I recall the story of a man walking along the beach and noticing only one set of footprints.

FOOTPRINTS

One night a man had a dream. He dreamed he was walking along the beach with the LORD. Across the sky flashed scenes from his life. For each scene, he noticed two sets of footprints in the sand: one belonged to him : and the other to the LORD.

When the last scene of his life flashed before him , he looked back at the footprints in the sand. He noticed that many times along the path of his life there was only one set of footprints. He also noticed that it happened at the very lowest and saddest times in his life.

This really bothered him, and he questioned the LORD about it. :LORD, you said that once I decided to follow you, you'd walk with me all the way. But I have noticed that during the most troublesome times in my life, there is only one set of footprints. I don't understand why when I needed you most you would leave me"

The LORD replied "My precious child, I love you and I would never leave you. during your times of trial and suffering, when you saw only one set of footprints, it was then that I carried you.

-Author Unknown

How I Got Over

How I got over
My soul looks back and wonders how I got over.
Soon as I see Jesus, the man that set me free.
The man that bled and suffered and died for you and me.
I thank him because he taught me.
Thank him because he brought me.
Thank him because he kept me.
Thank him cause he never left me.
I'm gonna sing (hallelujah)
I'm gonna shout (troubles over)
My soul looks back in wonders
How I got over
-Author Unknown

Hallelujah!
We will sing just as the birds in the early morning rise
Just as the sun between the clouds rise
Hallelujah!
Even the flowers have a time to rise
Our time will come when the dark cloud of grief rise
Hallelujah!
Oh, happy day my eyes will rise
To the heavens for the tears are gone
Joy is on the rise!
Hallelujah!
-Alicia

And God shall wipe away all tears from their eyes; and there shall be no more death, neither sorrow, nor crying, neither shall there be any more pain: for the former things are passed away.
Revelations 21:4 KJV

In his kindness God called you to share in his eternal glory by means of Christ Jesus. So after you have suffered a little while, he will restore, support, and strengthen you, and he will place you on a firm foundation.
1Peter 5:10 NLT

Alicia J Evans

<u>Note from the Author</u>

I began this journey after the passing of my mom, and I realized I had not gotten over losing my father and older sister. As time went on I continued to write and add as my family and friends continued to die. I eventually realized the longer I wait to finish *How I Got Over* I will continue adding names and stories. As my dear friend and sister Tawanna Sams reminded me, "the circle of life must continue. We are born to live, and then to die. That is called the circle of life."

My prayer is that my story helps someone. As my Aunt Edie the matriarch of my family who has recently gained her wings would say, "if I can help somebody then my living is not in vain."

If one person reaches out to me and shares how my story has helped them, then my living will not be in vain.

I pray that you are strengthened while reading these words.

Thank You, I Love You and I am praying for you and with you.

About The Author

Alicia J Evans finds joy in writing and telling stories. She believes there is something magical in weaving words together to tell a tale. Alicia loves reading, cooking and entertaining family and friends. She is a member of The Mount Olivet Baptist Church of Hollis where she enjoys worshiping and being of service.

Learn more about Alicia:
www.aliciajevans.com
Follow her on social media:
www.facebook.com/alicia.evans.35
Instagram: spin_a_tale2tell

Use this space to add the names of your loved ones. As you say their name we honor their memory.

How I Got Over

Made in the USA
Middletown, DE
26 July 2024